THE BOY WHO TURNED INTO A TV SET

Stephen Manes

Drawings by Michael Bass

AN AVON CAMELOT BOOK

For Esther

Coming Soon From Camelot Books By

Stephen Manes

HOOPLES ON THE HIGHWAY

STEPHEN MANES is a native of Pittsburgh, Pennsylvania, and studied at the University of Chicago and the University of Southern California. He has written for motion pictures and television. Mr. Manes currently lives in Riverdale, New York.

6th grade reading level has been determined by using the Fry Readability Scale

AVON BOOKS
A division of
The Hearst Corporation
1790 Broadway
New York, New York 10019

Text Copyright © 1979 by Stephen Manes
Illustrations Copyright © 1979 by Michael Bass
Published by arrangement with Coward, McCann & Geoghegan, Inc.
Library of Congress Catalog Card Number: 78-31436
ISBN: 0-380-62000-6

The Coward, McCann & Geoghegan, Inc. edition contains the following Library of Congress Cataloging in Publication Data:

Manes, Stephen.
  The boy who turned into a TV set.
  SUMMARY: Ogden Pettibone watched television so much that he finally turned into a set with the picture appearing on his stomach.
  [1. Television—Fiction] I. Bass, Michael. II. Title.
PZ7.M31264Bo   [Fic]   78-31436

First Camelot Printing, January, 1983

CAMELOT TRADEMARK REG. U.S. PAT. OFF. AND IN
OTHER COUNTRIES, MARCA REGISTRADA, HECHO EN U.S.A.

Printed in the U.S.A.

BAN   10 9 8 7 6 5 4 3

One

Ogden Pettibone watched television all the time. He watched game shows and news shows, police shows and educational shows, comedies and dramas, public service announcements, weather reports, cartoons, and commercials. Ogden would watch anything. Except soap operas. Ogden thought soap operas were dumb.

"If you keep watching TV so much," his mother often told him, "you might just turn into a television." Ogden always laughed when she said that. He knew she was only kidding. He knew people didn't really turn into TV sets.

One horrible day after school, Ogden came home to find that the Pettibones' television was broken.

"Broken!" he screamed. "How could it be broken?"

"It doesn't get a picture, and the only sound it makes is a sizzling noise, and smoke comes from the back when you turn it on," said his mother. "Someone will come out and fix it tomorrow."

"Tomorrow!" Ogden wailed. "But I need to watch my programs today!"

"Read a book for a change," Mrs. Pettibone suggested.

"Phooey," said Ogden, but he took his mother's advice. He went to the bookshelf and looked for a volume called *How to Repair Your Own TV*. Skimming through it, he found the information he was looking for. "No picture; sizzling, smoke: BIG TROUBLE. Do not attempt to fix this yourself, or you will be sorry. Unplug the set and call a repairman."

Ogden frowned, put the book back on the shelf, had some milk and cake, and watched his goldfish swim around the aquarium. It was slightly more interesting than staring at the blank TV screen.

"Dinnertime!" his father finally shouted from the kitchen.

Ogden opened his mouth to say he'd be right there, but instead a deep voice came out. "We'll be right back after this important message," it said. Ogden was very surprised.

"Don't be funny, Ogden," his dad scolded.

"I've never seen clothes so white!" Ogden exclaimed in a

woman's voice that startled him even more. "How do you do it?"

His mother frowned. "Og, what's wrong with you? Come to dinner while it's hot."

Ogden sat down at the table. "I use Ultra Wash," he said in another woman's voice. "It has twenty-seven percent more cleaning power." This wasn't what Ogden wanted to say at all. It was just what came out of his mouth when he opened it and tried to speak. He couldn't understand it.

"Enough, Ogden," said his father. "I don't think you're amusing."

Neither did Ogden. He felt as though he were a dummy on the lap of some invisible ventriloquist. "Ultra Wash gets your clothes so bright, your friends will not believe the sight!" a chorus sang cheerfully through his lips. Embarrassed, Ogden slumped down in his chair.

"Sit up straight and stop this foolishness," his mother commanded. "If you can't behave, you'll go up to your room without supper. Now, tell us what you did in school today."

Ogden thought he must be going crazy. He tried to tell them about the guinea pig that had triplets, but what came out of his mouth was someone else's voice saying, "Well, that just about wraps up our show."

"It certainly does!" snapped his mother. "Go up to your room, and don't come back till you're ready to behave."

Ogden wanted to protest. But when he opened his mouth, a voice said, "See you same time tomorrow."

"Get going! Right now!" his father shouted.

Ogden left the table. He plodded up the stairs and flopped down on his bed. "I can't understand it!" he said to himself, making very sure he didn't open his mouth. "What's happening to me?"

He let out a big sigh. Before he had a chance to finish it, a new voice squealed with glee. "Whee!" it exclaimed. "I've been chocolatized!"

Ogden clapped his hand over his mouth to keep anything else from coming out. Whatever was going on, it was worse than a bad case of hiccups.

In fact, it was a lot like hiccups. Ogden tried holding his breath. But after a while he began turning blue and had to come up for air. "Good evening," a robust voice said as Ogden gasped.

"President Ablefinger announced today that he believes more money should be spent on peanut butter research."

Ogden slammed his jaws shut. Maybe some water would help. He went to the bathroom and filled a cup. But as he opened his mouth to take a sip, he heard an elderly voice say, "False teeth a problem?" The water drowned the next words out, but when the glass was empty, the voice declared, "I can eat anything now!" and took a loud chomp on an invisible apple.

Hiccup cures didn't always work on Ogden's hiccups, and it was obvious they weren't going to work on this problem, either. He went into his bedroom, turned out the lights, lay down on his bed, closed his eyes, and tried to think.

It wasn't much use. He didn't have any idea what was the matter with him. And how could he explain his predicament to his parents if every time he opened his mouth, something stupid came out? He sighed again. "A swarm of giant fruit flies attacked the town of Quagmire, Montana, today," said his lips in a resonant baritone.

Ogden shut his mouth and opened his eyes. Suddenly he

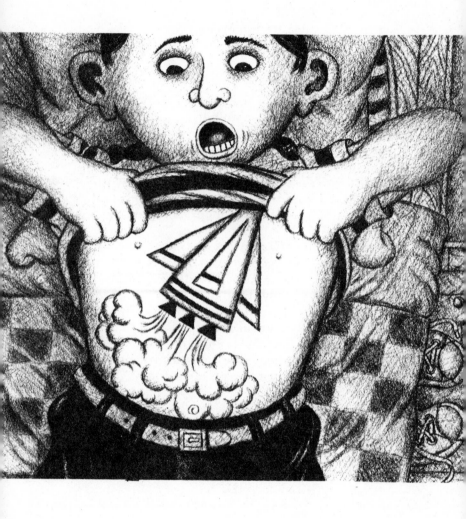

noticed that his T-shirt seemed to be glowing. He untucked it to take a closer look.

The T-shirt wasn't glowing at all. His stomach was. Right above his bellybutton was the six o'clock news in living color. A rocket on his tummy-screen blasted off toward his chest.

Ogden's jaw dropped in amazement, and he bellowed a deafening rocketlike roar. "Wow!" he thought. "I've turned into a TV!"

Two

Ogden's parents heard the blastoff.

"What's all that racket? Are you okay?" his father hollered, rushing up the stairs.

Ogden kept his mouth shut.

"Did you fall out of bed or something? What was all that noise?"

Ogden pointed to his belly. The rocket disappeared into the clouds.

"It's the six o'clock news!" his father cried. "But where's the sound?"

Ogden pointed to his mouth and opened wide. "Tomorrow, the astronauts will attempt the first game of baseball ever played in outer space," he said in the voice of the reporter who appeared on the screen. Then he closed his mouth again.

"Open up a minute," his father said. "I want to hear whether they caught those sneak thieves."

Ogden obediently loosened his jaws. The criminals were still at large, but the police had recovered the stolen truckload of tennis shoes.

"What's going on here?" Mrs. Pettibone wanted to know.

"Ogden's turned into a TV set," his father explained.

"I always said he would," his mother gloated.

"How did it happen?" his father asked him.

Ogden shrugged. He knew as little about it as they did.

"Well, enough's enough," said his mother. "Shut yourself off and come back down to dinner."

Ogden shook his head.

"Why not?" His father scowled.

Ogden grabbed a pad and pencil from his desk and scribbled the words, "I can't."

"Don't be ridiculous," his father said.

Ogden scribbled furiously. "I'm telling the truth," he wrote. "I don't know how this happened. I can't shut myself off. And I can't talk, because every time I open my mouth, TV sounds come out."

"Hmmmm," his father hummed thoughtfully.

"What shall we do?" his mother worried.

"I think we'd better have the doctor take a look at Ogden in the morning."

"And in the meantime?" Ogden wrote.

"Well, as long as our TV's broken, you might as well make yourself useful," his father replied. "Come downstairs and let us watch you."

Ogden ate supper. He felt rather uncomfortable making TV sounds between each bite, but his parents were very understanding.

Then they all went into the living room. Ogden sat in front of the broken television and took off his T-shirt. While his parents stared at him from the couch, he watched his amazing belly in a mirror at their feet. The mirror made the picture look backward, but he preferred that to the topsy-turvy view and stiff neck he got when he looked straight down at his screen.

"Excellent reception," said his father during a commercial break, "even though the picture is a bit small. And this remote control is the best yet. If we want the sound louder, all we have

to do is ask. Maybe we won't have to have our old set fixed after all."

"But Ogden only gets one channel," Mrs. Pettibone reminded her husband.

"Forgot about that," said Mr. Pettibone.

Ogden hoped they weren't serious. Much as he enjoyed being the center of attention, he still felt funny about his glowing stomach and contrary vocal cords. He hoped the doctor would be able to figure out what was wrong with him.

"Open up, dear," Mrs. Pettibone requested. "The commercial's over."

Ogden sighed into action.

Three

The new television did not sleep well that night. The glow from his screen didn't shine through the covers, but his mouth occasionally fell open as he dozed off, and then a loud commercial or an audience howling at a comedian's joke would waken him.

He was tired and hungry when he came down to breakfast, but his parents asked him not to eat until the commercials came on so that they wouldn't miss any of the morning news. Ogden obliged them, but he did feel rather chilly sitting at the table without a shirt on.

After breakfast, he and his father rode to the doctor's office on a bus. It was crowded, but they found two seats together, and everything was fine until Ogden yawned.

"I hate to be the one to tell you this," a girl's voice said through his mouth, "but you have bad breath."

"WHAT?" stormed the enormous woman beside him. "Who said that?"

"Bad breath," the voice repeated before Ogden could close his jaws.

"I do *not!*" the woman huffed. "I don't know who you think you are, but you had better apologize, sonny!"

Ogden would have liked to, but he knew there was no telling what might come out if he opened his mouth again. He kept it shut.

"Please excuse him," his father told the woman. "I'm sure he didn't mean it."

"Then why did he say it? The least he can do is apologize for himself."

"He really is sorry," said Mr. Pettibone. "Aren't you, Ogden?"

Ogden nodded.

"You didn't mean it, did you?"

Ogden shook his head.

"Humph," the woman sniffed, and turned away.

Just then the bus went over a bump in the road, jolting its passengers so violently that Ogden's jaw dropped open again.

"Do you have trouble losing weight?" asked an announcer's voice before Ogden could get himself under control.

The huge woman turned bright red and looked as though she might explode any second. Mr. Pettibone whisked his son to the exit, and marched him off the bus.

"I know it wasn't your fault," Mr. Pettibone told Ogden as they walked toward the doctor's office, "but please try to keep your mouth closed. We wouldn't want another unpleasant incident."

Ogden nodded and clenched his teeth.

The doctor's waiting room was filled with sick kids and their parents. Ogden found a book on airplanes and sat down beside his father to read it.

"My name's Jennifer," said a runny-nosed little girl who came up to him. "What's yours?"

Ogden didn't want to be unfriendly, but he thought he'd better not try to say anything.

"Hey! I said what's your name!"

Ogden just smiled, keeping his lips tight.

"Tell me your name!" the girl insisted, jumping in the air and landing right on Ogden's toes.

Ogden opened his mouth to say "Ow!" but what came out instead was a lionlike roar: "GRRRRRRRRRR!" It sounded so realistic, it scared little Jennifer back to her mother.

"Quite a cough your son has," commented the woman sitting next to Ogden's father. "I certainly hope it isn't contagious." Mr. Pettibone shook his head.

The nurse led Ogden and his father to an examining room. "The doctor will be with you shortly," she told Ogden. "Please take off all your clothes except your underpants."

Ogden did. He checked his screen. It was showing a soap opera, so he didn't bother to open his mouth to listen.

"Hello, Ogden," Doctor Stark said cheerfully when he came in a few minutes later. "What seems to be the trouble?"

Ogden pointed to the picture on his stomach. His father explained the problem.

"Hmmmm," said the doctor, bending over to take a look. "Unusual." He pointed a tongue depressor toward Ogden's mouth. "Say 'ah.' "

Ogden tried. What came out instead was a woman's voice saying, "I'm afraid there's not much hope for Penny after that terrible auto accident."

"Hmmmm," said the doctor again, and peered intently at Ogden's screen.

"Do you think it's serious?" his father asked.

"Oh, Penny will pull through," Doctor Stark reassured him. "She has to. She's the star of the show."

"But what about Ogden?" Mr. Pettibone wondered.

"Hmmmm," said Doctor Stark. He put his stethoscope in his ears and listened to his patient's chest, stomach, back, and neck. He examined Ogden's eyes and ears. Then he stuck a thermometer in Ogden's mouth and watched the soap opera for three minutes, even though he couldn't hear what the actors were saying, since Ogden had to keep his mouth closed. Finally Doctor Stark took the thermometer out again.

"No fever," he said. "Ogden, I'm afraid there's nothing I can do for you."

"But he can't even speak for himself," Mr. Pettibone protested. "Is it something like laryngitis?"

"It's a much more difficult case than that, I'm afraid. Ogden has televisionosis."

"Televisionosis?" Ogden wanted to ask. Mr. Pettibone asked it for him.

"Yes," Doctor Stark replied. "It's a disease so rare it's practically unheard of. I've certainly never heard of it before. One of my patients used to get radio stations on his tooth fillings, but this is much more severe. Your boy is exhibiting all the symptoms of a television set."

"But he doesn't want to be a television set."

"I'm afraid he has no choice. There's no known cure for televisionosis."

"Oh, my," said Mr. Pettibone, too stunned to say anything else.

"Perhaps he'll outgrow it," said the doctor pleasantly. "And if he doesn't, he'll be very popular. Everybody loves television."

Four

Ogden felt miserable. He didn't want to be a television the rest of his life, no matter how popular he might be. He decided he would pretend he was not a television, and he went to school that afternoon as if everything were normal.

But when his math teacher asked him what eleven times twelve was, Ogden told her in a very authoritative voice that she had smelly feet. She sent him to the principal's office.

When the principal asked him how he felt about what he'd done, Ogden whispered that she had perspiration odor. She made him stay late after school.

And when he got home and met his friends, Ogden told them matter-of-factly that they had ugly pimples. They refused to play with him. They wouldn't even look his way when he tried to show them his TV screen. Ogden whimpered like the hungry puppy who appeared on his belly, and sadly went home.

The TV repairwoman, Mrs. Turkel, was in the living room working on the broken set. Ogden watched her take it apart and replace some burnt-out tubes. Then she put it back together again. It worked beautifully.

Ogden suddenly had an idea. "Can you fix me, too?" he wrote on a scrap of paper. He handed it to the repairwoman and pulled up his T-shirt.

"Don't be silly, Ogden," Mrs. Pettibone scolded.

The repairwoman stared at Ogden's screen. "Perhaps there *is* something I can do," she said. "Open wide."

Ogden did. "And for a limited time only . . ."

"Close, please," Mrs. Turkel interrupted. Ogden obeyed.

"Your picture's perfect, and so's your sound," she told him. "What's the problem?"

"He doesn't want to be a television," Mrs. Pettibone explained.

"You don't?" exclaimed the repairwoman, shaking a finger at Ogden. "Why in the world not? Televisions are the greatest invention in the history of civilization. What other invention lets you watch old movies, bowling tournaments, and congressional hearings in the comfort of your own home while you eat a tuna fish sandwich? No other invention, that's what! You don't want to be a television? Try being a garbage disposer and see how you like that!"

Ogden could hardly say anything to disagree.

"At least he'd like to be able to change channels once in a while," said Mrs. Pettibone.

"Well, why didn't you say so?" said the repairwoman, taking a screwdriver from behind her ear. "Where's his channel selector?"

"That's just it," Mrs. Pettibone said. "I don't think he has one."

"Nonsense! Every television has one. You just have to know where it is."

Mrs. Turkel took her screwdriver and tapped it gently on Ogden's head. Nothing happened. She tapped his forehead. Still nothing happened. She poked his nose. Suddenly, the commercial on Ogden's screen disappeared, and a game show took its place. "Open wide, please," said the repairwoman. Ogden did.

"True or false? Every three-toed sloth actually has six

toenails," the quizmaster asked. The repairwoman poked Ogden's nose again.

The quizmaster disappeared, and a picture of a small living room took his place. "Ay-yi-yi!" hollered a funny-looking man who ran into the room and tore his hair. "How could a rhinoceros run into our car when it was in the garage all day?" An unseen audience screamed with laughter.

"Close, please," said Mrs. Turkel. Ogden did. He felt a little better. He still didn't like being a TV, but at least now he had a choice of programs.

"Well, that problem's solved," said Mrs. Turkel. "Anything else?"

"It would be nice if he could turn himself off some of the time," said Mrs. Pettibone. Ogden nodded agreement.

"Just use his switch," said Mrs. Turkel.

"But where is it?" Ogden's mother asked.

"Right here, of course," said the repairwoman, and she poked her screwdriver gently into Ogden's bellybutton. His picture suddenly disappeared, and his stomach looked exactly the way it used to, except for a little white dot in the middle. And that quickly faded, too.

By now Ogden was accustomed to keeping his mouth shut, since opening it usually seemed to get him into trouble, so it took him a little while to think of trying his voice again. "Does this mean I can talk?" he finally asked. His ears gave him the answer.

"Hooray!" he shouted. "I'm not a TV anymore!"

"Of course you are," said Mrs. Turkel. "Poke your belly-button and see for yourself."

Ogden did. His stomach lit up again, and his mouth said, "Never before and never again will this offer . . ." He poked his navel once more. The picture and sound cut off instantly.

"You see?" cried the repairwoman triumphantly. "You're as good a television as any I've ever fixed. *Now* how do you feel about it?"

Ogden wasn't a hundred percent sure. "Better, I guess. It sure is nice to have an off switch."

"Absolutely!" exclaimed the repairwoman. "Anyone who knows anything about televisions will tell you. That's the most important part!"

Ogden couldn't agree more.

Five

Now that he could turn himself on and off, Ogden rather enjoyed being a television, and he watched himself every chance he got. When he did something wrong, his parents couldn't punish him by making him miss his favorite programs. There were no more arguments when Ogden wanted to watch a documentary and his parents wanted to watch cartoons. And as Doctor Stark had predicted, Ogden soon became the most popular kid in his school. Everybody wanted to watch him, and he was delighted to have so many admirers.

His fame spread. TV reporters interviewed him. Newspapers wrote articles about him. And he appeared on the quiz show *Guess What I've Got*, along with a woman who had grown a radish shaped exactly like a dinosaur and a man who owned the world's largest chocolate-covered fish. Unlike the others, Ogden and his TV screen completely stumped the panel, and he won a lifetime supply of marshmallow chickens.

The owner of a department store spotted Ogden on the show and hired him to stand in a window after school and Saturdays alongside the sets the store had for sale. Ogden politely waved at the people who came to stare at him, and he was pleased when they noticed that his picture was by far the sharpest.

But soon he grew tired of being a television. The job in the window began to bore him. His new friends insisted on watching him on the way to school, and when the weather turned cold, he got goose bumps from having nothing on his tummy but a picture. The kids always argued about which programs they should watch, so Ogden's nose soon turned a deep red from their repeated pokings.

Soon Ogden was so sick of being a television, he wouldn't even *watch* TV. He wouldn't sit in the room while his parents watched. He wouldn't even glance at his favorite programs. Finally, he turned himself off and put a piece of tape over his navel so that no one could turn him on.

The store owner was sorry to lose his best attraction. The disappointed kids called their former friend "Ogden the Oddball" and "Obnoxious Ogden" and "Telly-Belly." Mr. and

Mrs. Pettibone were concerned. They knew something was wrong with their son, but they didn't know exactly what.

On Thanksgiving Day, Ogden stayed in his room and read a book about monsters instead of watching the annual parades. But late that afternoon, his father shouted from the living room, "Ogden! Come here! Quickly!"

It sounded like an emergency, so Ogden hurried as fast as he could. When he got downstairs, he saw smoke coming from the back of the television set as his father unplugged it.

"Our TV just broke again! The football game's tied with seconds to play!" Mr. Pettibone shouted. "Turn yourself on! Hurry!"

Ogden knew how much football meant to his father. He pulled up his sweater, ripped off the adhesive tape, and poked himself in the bellybutton.

Nothing happened.

"Maybe you didn't press hard enough," his father said, and gave Ogden's navel a healthy poke. Ogden grunted, but nothing appeared on his tummy.

"I don't know what's wrong!" Ogden cried, poking his midriff frantically. "I worked the last time I tried."

"Never mind," said his father. "The game's probably over anyhow. We'll have Mrs. Turkel fix the TV in the morning. Maybe she can fix you, too."

"Not me!" Ogden shouted. "I'm tired of being a TV."

"There's just no pleasing some people," said his mother, shaking her head.

Ogden couldn't believe his nightmare was over. Every few minutes he would poke his bellybutton to make sure, and each time he was delighted when absolutely nothing happened. But now that it was over, he didn't really regret having been a TV. After all, how else would he ever have won a lifetime supply of marshmallow chickens?

At dinner, Ogden silently gave thanks that he wasn't a television anymore. Then he had five helpings of turkey.

"My word, Ogden!" cried his mother when he asked for a sixth. "If you keep eating turkey, you might just turn into a turkey!"

Ogden laughed. He knew she was only kidding. He knew people didn't really turn into turkeys.

But just to be on the safe side, he passed up another helping and saved room for dessert.